W9-DIB-989

Other books by the author:

The High Traverse, novel

CARE GIVER

Richard Blanchard

Livingston Press
The University of West Alabama

isbn 13: 978-1-60489-112-6, hardcover
isbn 13: 978-1-60489-113-3, trade paper
isbn: 1-60489-112-2, hardcover
isbn: 1-60489-113-0, trade paper
Library of Congress Control Number 2013930862
Printed on acid-free paper.
Printed in the United States of America by
United Graphics
Hardcover binding by: HF Group Bindery
Typesetting and page layout: Joe Taylor
Cover layout and design: Joe Taylor
Cover photo: Richard Blanchard
Proofreading: Michael Kimberly, Melissa LaFond

A Salute to Gordon Lish.

Another thanks to Joe Taylor,

and with gratitude to David Lister,

Jim Mizer, and to Darrell and Mike.

Livingston Press is part of The University of West Alabama,
and thereby has non-profit status.
Donations are tax-deductible.
first edition
6 5 4 3 3 2 1

CARE GIVER

For
M a r g o

Be thou faithful unto death, and
I will give thee the crown of life.

The Revelation of John 2:10

My name is John.

One of my jobs was to deliver newspapers and magazines to the old folks after school. I was doing my rounds at the Spring Lake Home on the day they were cleaning out his room for the next patient, and that's when they gave me his album and his notebook with the letters he never mailed.

I've made notes about what happened every day as best as I can remember. Please read what he wrote to her and what I've added to his notebook. I've tried hard to put everything in the right order.

Now I need to get the cottage ready before she comes back home.

Dear Margo,

My room is a single. I am almost eighty-one. What happens happens in the night, but in the daytime, too. I'll try to write you every morning. They take care of us. It's hard for me to concentrate on one thing at a time. I look at your picture. Nighttime is the best. The paper boy comes after school. They keep our windows shut. I am waiting for you. They are giving me more tests. I'm every age I've ever been.

Yours forever,

Bob

He told me his name was Bob Brown the first day I remember seeing him. He had an album open on the bed and he was looking at a newspaper clipping of a young woman.

Dear Margo,

We were alone out on the porch. Pop let me take the car. They sit me up in bed like this so I can write this down. You had the Victrola playing. School was over with. Your mother made iced tea for us. "Want to dance?" you said. My hands were folded on my knees. Your mother said good night. Sometimes I try not to think. The moon and stars were out. "Let me show you," you said. The porch light was turned off. Someone in the next room's shouting "God, please help me, please!" You put my hand behind your back. I stood up good and straight. They change our sheets on Wednesday. Your breath was sweet mint tea. "Like this," you said. The next song came on. We have doctors here. I'm trying to write this exactly how it was last night. You had your arm around me. We were moving back and forth. They shave me every morning. Our cheeks touched. My homework's done. Breakfast is served early. You showed me another step. The nurse gives us our morning pills. I saw your dark eyes. It was late. We did not stop. Your lips moved on my cheek. Most Protestants don't wear a cross, but I do anyway. I heard you whisper something. The bathroom's down the hall. We go to church on Sunday. You held me closer in. They put my things in storage. You took me by the hand. Everything gets done for us here. We stepped through the door. My truck is somewhere up on blocks. I followed you inside. We tiptoed up the inside stairs. I could hear my heart. Is that breakfast coming? I'm B-42. This is how it was last night. Remember?

Yours,

Bob B.

B – 42 Album
Newspaper clipping
No identification

Care Giver

Let me tell you more.

He left what he called "...all (his) worldly goods and possessions" to <u>me</u>, and I was just a boy who first got to know him when I delivered papers and magazines to his room at the Spring Lake Home.

Dear Margo,

"Date of birth?" the doctor asked. Yes, I remembered
that. It was just this morning. The nurse was watching
me. "Name of father?" he said. I didn't answer yet. He took
notes. I saw her moving dials on a machine. "Your age?"
he said. That was easy. "This won't hurt," she said. We
have a dementia wing here at the Spring Lake Home. She
put her hand upon my shoulder. "Next of kin?" he said.
Her hair was in a ponytail. I said Margo Jones. "Military
service?" He was writing all this down. "11329321," I said.
"PFC." She touched me. "Month of the year?" I could have
answered that. She slid her fingers down my arm and
stopped where my wrist is. I heard the Victrola. She was in
your summer blouse. "Our country's President?" She was
turning switches on. "Your mother's name? Room number?"
I couldn't think of them. She attached a wire. I breathed in
sweet mint tea. She put her arm around my back. I say my
prayers at night. She stood close. This room is warm. You

switched the porch light out. "Your name?" Of course. She held my hand. A screen was lighting up. You made believe you were the nurse, but I knew.

Yours,

Bob B.

He was a nice old man who seemed lonely, and one night I had a dream about him. The two of us were hiking together on a trail somewhere up in the mountains, and he was leading the way. That was all there was.

The next day I asked one of the nurses more about him. She told me that she remembered a young woman had come to visit him once. All she could remember was that she was tall and that she had dark hair.

Dear Margo,

It was snowing. It was dark. The phone book's by my bed. I had to find the cottage! You were waiting for me there. My phone is a rotary. I thought I saw a light! The snow was getting deeper. There was nothing else in sight. It must have been fifteen below. I saw the cottage there! This phone book's got the yellow pages and the white combined. I bundled up. It's way up there. My watch doesn't work. I can read the small print if I hold it close enough. Everything looked different. My boots got filled with snow. I've checked the yellow pages. A window was lit up! There is a Churches section. I trudged up to the porch. This didn't look like our place. They have Baptist; Church of Christ. I knocked. You didn't answer. Jehovah's Witnesses. I peered in through the window and I saw someone inside! It hasn't snowed here at Spring Lake. The Christmas tree was lit. I could smell a wood fire. The glass was frosted up. You were sitting by the fire! I know the paper boy. Methodist;

Pentacostal. It looked warm inside. Why didn't you see me out there? First Episcopal. I couldn't feel my hands and feet. Presbyterian. I rubbed frost off the window. The storm did not let up. You had a blanket 'round you but I think you were undressed. I hear Him in the mountains. The porch light was off. I saw two cups by the fire. The front door was locked. I checked the white pages. Your name is not there. I saw a cross up on the wall beside the Christmas tree. My name is not listed either. You were all alone. I kept knocking and stood out there in the cold.

Yours,

Bob

I also asked about him at the Spring Lake administration office. The secretary pulled his file out and told me that his full name was Robert A. Brown. She also said his previous address was missing, but that his next of Kin was listed as Margo Jones with no address written in. She said that the Spring Lake Home held a bank account in his name to draw upon as needed for his care.

Then I checked through the local phone book to see if I could find anyone in his family. Brown is a common name, but there was only one Robert A. Brown listed. I called that number, and they had never heard of the Robert A. Brown at Spring Lake Home. I called other Browns, but they didn't know him either. Then I called 411. They didn't have a listing for any other Robert A. Brown or for a Margo Jones. I made a note to try to find old phone books to see if they were listed years ago.

Dear Margo,

Last night I was driving there. The road got very steep. My wheelchair comes with footrests. I saw snow up ahead. They put a cushion in my wheelchair. I had four-wheel drive. The road turned into gravel. I knew I had to get through. It got higher with each switchback. I dropped into low. They put in ramps and railings for us here at Spring Lake Home. My tires were good. I hugged the cliff. The pass was just ahead. I can wheel myself around. The Jeep was running hot. It got even steeper. The cliff dropped off below. There are handles on my chair in case I need a push. I know I saw you through the window. The gas gauge said E. Was it someone else's cottage? I can walk myself. The bumper scraped the uphill side. I made it to the pass! "Easy does it," I said. My wheelchair comes with brakes. The road had gotten icy. Your mother was asleep. Our bus comes with a wheelchair lift to get us on and off. The other side was even steeper. I pumped on the brakes. They strap us in to make sure we don't fall and hurt ourselves. The road got very narrow. It was getting dark. Everything I need at Spring Lake Home is on this floor. I kept going faster! My brakes hit the floor! We've got special beepers on our wheelchairs just in case. I couldn't stop! The brakes were burning! It turned to a trail! You put your arms around me. They say safety first. I couldn't even see the trail. My steering wheel broke off! The Jeep was bouncing, sliding, faster! We were by ourselves. I careened out to the brink! Your cheek touched my face. Someone shouted "It's okay…wake up." The nurse was here. Dear Margo, I am in my room. Don't let the doctor know. I am waiting for tonight. She checked my pulse.

Yours,

B.

The nurse also told me that he had hallucinations in the night, and that counseling from the Spring Lake psychologist did not seem to help.

Dear Margo,

"Prostate enlarged," the doctor says. I feel better now. The doctor says the prostate is what cuts down on the flow. The nurses talk like I'm not here. Pop let me take the car. Our prostate glands do not stop growing, so the doctor says. They must think that I'm asleep. My PSA is up. They check for prostate cancer. It was dark out on the porch. It's hard for me to hold it in. The nurses check my chart. "Not too loud, we'll wake him up," I heard one of them say. The doctor felt inside me. "He's so quiet," one nurse said. C-4 had prostate surgery. Your lips touched my cheek. "He's always writing," one said. I kept my eyes shut. The doctor said C-4 has lost the feelings that he had. One nurse said "Who's he writing to?" Your mother went to bed. It happens to most older men. I can't sleep through the night. "He writes in his notebook." They could do a biopsy. "His writing's hard to read," one said. "The words are all mixed up." "His chart says 'Under Observation,'" one said. School was out. We were alone out on the porch.

"Alzheimer's?" one nurse said. What? I bolted upright. They stopped talking about me. The doctor says I'm too old now for surgery.

Love,

B.

He always smiled at me and said "Hello, son" when I delivered the paper. Sometimes he also picked out a magazine to read, especially if it was large print, and whenever he finished he would give it back to me so I could pass it on to someone else.

One day he asked me how old I was. I was only seventeen then.

Dear Margo,

I've gotten back from rehab. It was just the two of us. I looked up the word "Alzheimer's." They said I'm strong enough. She stood me up. I held on. She kept me up straight. I checked off the list of symptoms: Memory loss? Not me. She got me set up for stretches. They have fresh-squeezed juice. Forgetting simple words? Not me. Her hands touched my leg. She wears shorts and T-shirt. Argumentative? Not me. Her teeth are going to look perfect with her braces off. "Good work, Mr. B," she said. She knows who I am. The paper boy comes every day. She held my ankles down. Needs close supervision? She put me in place. I do what she says to. Worried or depressed? Not me. I can do a sit-up. Losing things? Not me. Trouble recognizing friends? Could that be me? Could be. Next we did the catback stretch. Loss of interest? No. She put her hand behind my back. Her hair is dark like yours. Wanders at night? Yes, that's me. Her breath was sweet mint tea. We did the prone extension. Problems with the language? Yes? She put her legs against me. No one else was watching us. Believes that things are real when they are not? Could that be me? She shifted our position. I kept up. Our legs were one. "That's it for today," she said. Repeats himself? I do. Visions? Is that me? I see whatever He decides. Alzheimer's? There's no cure. Was that you in disguise?

Love,

B.

I looked up "Alzheimer's" for myself after I peeked at his chart and it said "Possible Alzheimer's."

I wonder if the doctors ever saw the letters he wrote. I don't think so.

Dear Margo,

We went back at our place. The trail came to an end. Spring Lake has got an air conditioner in every room. The sun was out. We've got TV. The creek was running deep. They installed venetian blinds. We filled our canteens up. The thermostat is on the set. Our sky was crystal clear. It must have sprinkled in the night. You led the way on up. Here comes the man who mops the floor. You knew where we were. The snowcapped peaks rose up on high above the valley floor. They keep it in the seventies. It was spring up there. Our radiator settings are controlled by management. The breeze was blowing from the south. You had your white blouse on. They keep extra blankets in the closet just in case. The meadow grass was lush and green. We had money saved. Antelope bobbed off across the meadow to the trees. My bed is adjustable. The mountain air was cool. This button rings a bell down where the nurses' station is. Meadow blossoms were in bloom. We breathed in heaven's scent. They put a humidifier in each patient room. I picked a blossom for you. A crane poked through the grass. I held the cross up to my lips. This room is ten by twelve. We stayed up in the high meadow. They say rain today. We were close to Him up there. Someone's coming now. We didn't want to start back down. They give me extra juice. I'm never sure where we are going until dark.

Love,

B.

Right now I'm looking at her picture in the newspaper clipping from his album. I look and look again.

Dear Margo,

What happened last night? I don't know. They gave me a
new pill. From now on I'll just make believe I swallowed it.

Yours,

B.

Some days he was sound asleep when I stopped at his room. I think this was one of those days.

Dear Margo,

Last night I was in fourth grade! You weren't watching
me. I could fly! They just came in to plug in my new phone. I
zoomed in for a landing. Other children gathered 'round. It's
the latest model. The new phone works hands-free. They said
I'm under observation. Miss Wright left the room. I leaped out
through the window and on up into the sky! This phone is a
speaker phone. I had x-ray eyes! They were talking all about
me. You were in pigtails. I could hear from anywhere. They
called me Wonder Boy. It's got what they call Caller I.D. I could
halt a train. Rockefeller knew me. I could see through women's
clothes. It takes a message for me if I don't pick up the phone.
I could catch a speeding bullet. I knocked out The Champ. I
looked to see if you were watching. I signed autographs. I can
take two calls at once. The President asked me. This phone's
got Call Waiting but I'm not sure what it is. Miss Wright came
back into class. I fought crime at night. You talked to another
boy. I called your number up. "Disconnected," it said. I called

information next. They asked me to translate the scrolls. "No listing, sir," they said. I kept knocking on the door. You must have a phone! I went back to the window. You were in there by yourself. Einstein asked me questions. Call Waiting has not lit. I haven't heard the phone ring yet.

Yours forever,

Bob

B – 42 Album
Handwriting on back of photo:
"Me – Miss Wright's class"

Care Giver

He was right. I remember when they installed those new speaker phones in all the rooms in the B-wing.

I wrote to the phone company to ask about their records of old listings for a Margo Jones or a Robert A. Brown. They never answered me.

Dear Margo,

They sent me out to find you. There was danger everywhere. I watch TV before lights out. It was a foreign land. I saw empty barstools. They said you were in disguise. This lever here adjusts my bed. A man was watching me. They had music playing. I tossed greenbacks on the bar. The nurse took blood this morning. My revolver did not show. The clock was moving backward. I saw dancers on the floor. They said you got the message. My sink is over there. I saw the barman staring. They couldn't see my cross. I ordered whiskey in their tongue. Was that you over there? There wasn't much time left for us. I squinted through the smoke. My bed tray rolls across the bed so I can write right here. You were dressed in native dress. One man was at the door. My uniform was hidden. The boy brings me magazines. You took a stool beside me! Another man came in. I try not to write these words 'til the beats come out right. The porch was stacked with firewood. I banged on the cottage door. You need a special key to get to the dementia wing. The music stopped. You whispered something. I lit up a light. "Be careful," you said. They were watching. Dancers left the floor. "They know about us," you said. Your blouse had come undone. I wear the cross beneath my robe to keep me safe and sound. They started coming toward us. Do I watch too much TV? "Follow me," you whispered. "We can make it..."

Love,

Bob B.

B – 42 Album
Newspaper clipping
No identification

Care Giver

This note was taped to the top of his album when
they gave it to me:

Please give these photos and my notebook
to our paper boy John Fulton when I am
gone.

Thank you.
Robert Brown
B-42

Dear Margo,

We hiked up together. You went first again. My calendar
is by the bed, but I can reach from here. We got up to the high
meadow. Pooch was with us, too. I mark the days off. It was
sunny. You were in your shorts. My watch is in safekeeping.
The porch light was turned off. We beheld the valley and the
meadow and the creek. I didn't say a thing at first. The breeze
was south again. I forgot to mark today off. It's October now. I
think He was looking down. You're darker than I am. We both
gazed up toward Him. The cottage will be here. I keep track
of every day. We drank from the creek. Pooch waded in beside
us. It was springtime out. We saw a trail up to the snowfields.
Wild flowers were in bloom. Antelope went bounding by. Pooch
barked. I held him back. We rested on our backpacks. I can't
read what day it is. We munched on our fruit and bread. I
braided up your braids. The boy can mark today off. I thanked
Him up above. "Where would you live?" I said, "if it could
be anywhere?" "Bobby," she said. "We're right here." I hear

sounds down the hall. It's hard to know where we will be until it's night again. This is the place. He knows we're here. You took me by the hand. They're coming in to make my bed and bring my pills.

Yours,

B.

Now I know what he was writing about, now that I've seen so many of those clear spring days up in the high meadow.

Dear Margo,

It was your birthday. I'm not there! My backpack disappeared. They've got me on other pills. My pack is navy blue. They take my blood pressure. The bus was loading up. I know how to check my pulse rate like the nurses do. It was dark out on the porch. My wallet was gone, too! The clock they put up in my room has a sweep second hand. I couldn't pay the bus fare. No one was helping me. I count my beats per minute. It was raining out. I looked for a phone booth. My heart beats are up. Maybe I could hitchhike. Your lips touched my cheek. You were waiting for me. I dug for some change. The heart keeps beating one strong beat, one soft beat, back and forth. The bus was ready to pull out. All my change was gone! I write extra large so I can read what I write down. "All aboard," the driver said. I was soaking wet. The driver pulled the bus door closed and wouldn't let me on. I started walking. No one stopped. My new phone doesn't work! I saw a cross beside the road and sat down next to it. "Margo, I'm right here," I said. The new pills don't help yet. A car was stopping! It was you! My heart won't slow down.

B

I've tried to do the arithmetic. He said he was almost eighty-one when he started writing the letters. If he and Margo were seventeen when they were together, that was 64 years ago! I called the marriage license bureau to see what I could find out, but no luck. The files before 1960 were lost when the old courthouse burned down.

Dear Margo,

It was a masquerade last night. I'm B-42. People had their costumes on, but I was only me. We were in the party room. I was by myself. Spring Lake Home looks after us. Tables said "Reserved." Our Father who art in heaven. I kept my wheelchair brakes on. They pay the bills from an account. Women were dressed up. Rehab is included. I thought maybe I saw you! They say we should not keep cash. I had my good clothes on. Prescription bills are extra. Was that you behind a mask? They didn't give a costume to me. I pulled up my socks. She started coming toward me. Local calls are free. They charge for special nursing care. I brushed back my hair. She was waving to me! Hallowed be Thy name. B-42 is written on the medicine I take. She came up beside me. They were watching us. She held my hand. "I've missed you," she said. I saw her brown eyes. Your mother made mint tea for us. "Masks off!" somebody said. She was an old woman I had never seen before. The nurse helped me back down the hall. I'll wait until tonight. You might think I'm just an old man living in my dreams. I <u>am</u> an old man writing this. But that's not all it is. I'm keeping track. The paper boy is good to me.

Love,

B.

Sometimes he asked me questions about myself. One day he said "What do you want to be, boy?"

I'd been thinking about that myself. "I'd like to get a good job when I finish school and save up money so someday I can have my own place," I said. "Right now Grandma and I just live in town."

He listened and he nodded. Then I think he asked me if I could help fix the pillow behind his back, and so I did.

Dear Margo,

What a night! The plane was diving. I heard screams and shouts. Our TVs have remote controls. Bags tumbled down the aisle. A warning signal sounded off. The plane was pulling out! I can turn the TV on from right here on my bed. A soldier hero's on the screen. I heard a baby cry. The stewardess grabbed me by the arm. "They're dead up there!" she said. I unhooked my safety belt. "It's up to you!" she said. I watch TV while I am writing. We veered left and right. The soldier's finally coming home. They've got banners out. I peered through the window. We were just above the trees! "You're our only chance," she said. He's looking for his girl. A woman made the sign of the cross. He's in uniform. The cockpit door was open. I crawled up the aisle. The soldier thinks he sees her! Your porch light was off. The pilots were slumped over. I've never flown a plane. She rushes past the soldier into someone else's arms. We dragged the bodies from the cockpit. Ads come on TV. The stewardess said "You've got to save us!" I took the controls.

Ads are still on. I strapped in. The stewardess had dark eyes. All those knobs and lights and gauges blinked in front of me. I squinted through the windshield. There were buildings just ahead! I tried to put us in a climb. Red lights went on and off. The soldier's back on. He's alone. The yoke broke in my hands! We were flying down a street with buildings on both sides! I click the remote control. The wings were breaking off! We kept flying anyway. I gained altitude! The stewardess took me by the hand. I looked, and she was you! The nurse is coming in now. I switch off TV.

Yours,

Bob

The next day he was still thinking about our talk. "I grew up in town, too," he said. "Pop took me to the mountains, and when we . . ." That's when the doctor came in and looked over at me and I knew it was time for me to leave.

Later, after he had passed away, one of the nurses let me see his medical record. It showed that they discontinued a drug called Valium and replaced it with another drug called Zoloft. I wrote it all down.

Dear Margo,

This time I was naked! The crowd was closing in. I get taken to the tub room every other day. They had sticks. They were shouting. It was freezing cold. She wheels me in. I was cornered. She takes off my robe. The crowd kept getting bigger. I tried to cover up. She fills the tub. She tests the water. They were calling names. I was thin and barefoot. All I had on was my cross. She helps me in. They had clubs. The water's nice and warm. My back was back against the wall. "This way...," someone said. The alley was behind me. She soaps me up and down. They threw rocks and bottles. "Look out!" I heard you say. Something hit me. I was bleeding. "Over here!" you said. The tub has got a shower. There you were behind a door! I broke loose. They lunged at me! You were naked, too! My feet were sticking to the ground. "Follow me!" you said. We ducked in through a hidden arch. She scrubs me everywhere. They rushed by. "Shhh...," you said. I hid behind the wall. She takes the shampoo from the shelf. I heard their screams and shouts. Your skin was olive. I held on. "In here," you said to me. We slipped through a secret door. She rubs the lather in. We were in a garden. There was a waterfall. We bathed in deep warm waters. Good Lord, thank you for this all. We get the tub room to ourselves. We rinse. She dries me off. I close my eyes and see you doing everything.

        Yours,

        B.

I think he was asleep when I got to his room the next day. The covers were halfway off his bed, and he looked so thin and so still that I stopped to make sure he was okay. I pulled the covers back up over him and left the paper by his bed where he would find it when he woke up.

Dear Margo,

It was steep! I was climbing. You were down below. My walker's got two legs on wheels, and two legs slide on skids. No one else was up there. I was almost high enough. They stand me up beside my walker. It's called Devil's Chute. I kicked in the footholds. You watched. My crampons held. I grip the walker with both hands. They say to hold on tight. I kept climbing. Left foot, right foot. I talk to myself. You could see where I was with my new red parka on. The skis were in my backpack. It got steeper every step. I get out of bed myself. "Don't stop now," I said. I go to the john alone. The chute looked like a wall. I can do the whole length of the Wing B hall myself. "Careful...," I said. I was counting. Almost to the top! I've seen the bodies of good climbers come careening down. My walker's got no-slip hand grips. "Fill your lungs...," I said. I can stand up from my wheelchair with no one to help. "You can do it!" I said. They don't lock my safety belt. "Slip the boots

into the bindings. Kick the snow off first." I was ready. "Now!"
I said. I looked down. It was steep! "Do it now! No! Yes! No!
Yes!" I set my wheelchair brakes. You were watching. "Ready!"
I said. "Okay. All set. Go!" I lost my balance. They caught me!
I shouldn't tell.

Love,

B.

He picked out my favorite ski magazine one day when I stopped by on my rounds. The next time I brought him old copies of <u>Ski and Mountaineering</u> and <u>Popular Science</u> that I had been saving in my room. Later on I gave him the magnifying glass I had gotten for Christmas after I saw him holding the magazines up so close to his face.

The next letter in his notebook said "Dear Margo," but the rest of the page was blank.

Later, when I got to see his medical record, one entry listed 2 mg of Clonazepam administered to B-42 every three hours starting at 2 p.m. until 2 p.m. the next day. It may have been on this day.

Dear Margo,

We have Sunday service. I went back to your old house. The minister knows who I am. Everything looked small. I stood up on the front steps. There was a light inside. They help me dress up for chapel in my Sunday clothes. I rang the bell. A man came. They had put on a new roof. Spring Lake is Presbyterian, but they let others in. The trees out front had gotten big. Our chapel's near Wing B. "May I help you?" the man said. They put in flower beds. I go every Sunday. The pew is up in front. "My girl grew up in this house," I said, "a long time ago." We do Bible readings. The man let me come inside. "Don't let me disturb you," I said. It looked different now. We just had the sermon. He stood by the stairs. The minister spoke of our loved ones in the afterlife. There's a house in your back yard. The porch is closed in now. I haven't told the minister what happens in the night. We tiptoed in. You took my hand. Your mother was asleep. "May I see her room?" I said. The man said yes I could. I looked. Your bed! Your desk! Your window! It was still right there. I saw our picture on your desk. Hallowed be Thy name. They wheeled me back to 42. Your breath was sweet mint tea. I look outside my window and I see a cross.

Yours,

B.

Photo found in Fulton cottage
Handwritten note on back:
"From the window of B – 42"

I forgot to tell you. He also kept The Bible and a dictionary in his bedside drawer. I have them now.

Dear Margo,

I've got too much time to think. My eyesight's getting worse. The boy leaves me good magazines for me to read in bed. I turn up the TV. They gave me a test. The title of one story is "Why Don't They Answer Us?" The print is big enough for me. They mean the universe. I haven't told them you come back here almost every night. They say that I've got cataracts. I turn the lights on high. It says our galaxy has been here for twelve billion years. They say my hearing's gotten worse, too. I'm okay at night. It says that Earth's a tiny dot in the whole galaxy. They put some old men in diapers. Medicaid might help. It says that there may be more than two hundred billion stars. They say my cataracts are ready. It is up to me. They're looking for who else is out there in the universe. I say not to fix them. They've got antennas up. There might be a zillion other planets in the sky. I smell mint tea in my room. Strong coffee still tastes good. It says we're sending signals, but no one has answered yet. They say Mars is the closest. I believe in UFOs. They're building space transmitters to send stronger signals out. Cataracts don't matter. I see you no matter what. They don't mention Him.

Yours forever,

Bob

I think he read every article in <u>Popular Science</u> magazine.

In science class we had been reading about tiny particles called living protons. The book said that we're all made up of protons and that our protons can be in more than one place at the same time.

Dear Margo,

I made a reservation. We get three meals a day. You looked as pretty as an actress. We eat early here. I double-checked my wallet. The head waiter had my name. Meals are included. The waiter called me "sir." We get fresh juice in the morning. I pulled back your chair. My shoes were shined. Pop's car was washed. Breakfast is at eight. I did not know how to start. "Wine list?" the man said. Our trays come on heated carts. I straightened up my tie. They say I'm losing too much weight. You had high heels on. I got to your house too early, so I drove around. They put me on a special menu. I wore my good suit. We had a tablecloth and napkins. Coffee clears my head. The waiter lit the candles. You had your hair just right. The menu wasn't English. They put butter on my toast. I didn't know what I should order. Lunch is 12 o'clock. The waiter made suggestions. You had your blue dress on. Our beds come with safety bars. Your mother made mint tea. I got our reservation more than two weeks in advance. It was all expensive. Supper comes at 6 p.m. You went to the ladies room and put more lipstick on. The ring was in my pocket. I looked left and right. My supper tray has meat balls, noodles, coffee, ice cream, cake. I slipped the ring onto your finger. My plate was not touched. Sometimes I look into the mirror and see someone else. Dear Margo, my cup runneth over. You said yes to me. Now we are forever. I can't eat.

Yours,

Bobby B.

One day he said "Have you got a girlfriend, son?" All I could say was "No"! (I didn't say how hard it was to talk to girls.)

Dear Margo,

Last night I ate all my supper. Your porch light was off. Our bus is wheelchair friendly. I signed up. They put me on. Your mother went upstairs to bed. I had a window seat. There was music playing. I wiped my glasses off. "Want to dance?" you said. The bus was slowing down. A man in the seat next to me had oxygen turned on. We waited for the light to change. It seemed like summer out. I saw a convertible. She sat close to him. Her hair was dark. The top was down. She was in her blouse. I could see them well enough from up there where I was. The traffic stopped. "Like this," you said. He was behind the wheel. She was over on his side. They stopped next to us. The other cars weren't moving. School was over with. It was dark out on the porch. Your cheek touched my face. Did I take my morning pills? One hand was on his knee. We were touching head to foot. They had snacks on the bus. Your lips were moving on my cheek. She looked up. She saw me! I heard you whisper something. My prescriptions help. She waved to me! I waved back. You had me by the hand. I saw the cars begin to move. You said "Follow me." They were pulling up ahead! Your breath was sweet mint tea. Dear Margo, our bus couldn't keep up! I'll wait.

Love,

B.B.

I didn't tell him that I had written a note to a girl I liked, and that I was still hoping she would answer me. (I'm still not sure that she ever knew my name.)

Dear Margo,

We pitched our tent beside the creek. It was summertime. The high meadow sparkled in the dew and morning light. We cleared the trail all the way up. It got cool at night. We cut back the branches where the old switchback road was. It got warm in the sunshine. We hauled the wagon up. Antelope were grazing. The high meadow was in bloom. We loaded boulders from the creek. You called me Mountain Bob. I picked a wild flower for you. Pooch was with us, too. Your hair was in the ponytail. We had all summer off. The cottage was staked out up there where the high meadow is. We dug for the footings. The creek ran cool and deep. We set stones and boulders for the new foundation walls. I worked on the chimney. We got up when it got light. I knew He was helping to make sure we did it right. We trimmed logs. We raised walls. You helped me hoist the beams. Our bedroom window faces east toward where the sun comes up. The big room has a high peak roof. Snowfields rose above. You said "Let's never leave here, Bobby." He was good to us. This was it. "Yes," I said. If only it will be. The nurse said that they're taking me for tests today.

Yours,

B.

He must have been thinking about the night before when he saw me the next day.

"We've got a spread out west of here," he told me. "Out by the high peaks, up where the snowfields are. I'll take you out there someday, son...".

"You've got your own land out there?" I asked him.

He nodded. "The next outfit is grazing it now," he said, "ever since I've been laid up..."

Dear Margo,

Last night I went to the parade. There goes our fire alarm! I was looking everywhere. They had a marching band. So far nobody looked like you. Main Street was roped off. The alarm bell for Wing B is just outside my room. I was taking snapshots. It must be another drill. Firecrackers got set off. No smoking is allowed. I saw a girl with your dark eyes. Each wing has fire drills. Someone let balloons loose. She was with somebody else. Flags were flying. I edged in. They were holding hands. It's hard to write with the bell ringing. He was hugging her. They're supposed to wheel me out. She was in her shorts. Veterans were marching by in their old uniforms. She was taller than he was. Kids were running by. She waved to the soldiers. I saw twirling majorettes. The exit signs are lighted. A prom queen threw a kiss. I stood at attention to salute the U.S. flag. The exit is just down the hall. We have drills every month. Whistles blew. Her hair was dark. Old men brought folding chairs. I had my camera ready. The mayor's float went by. They didn't see me watching. There're no sprinklers in the rooms. They were shooting water pistols. No one's come for me. She was getting closer. I clicked. I clicked again. A fire engine tooted. Her hair was pinned back. She looked directly at me! A cherry bomb went off. I guess the drill is over. There are people in the hall. She reached out and touched me but they kept on going by. I tried to catch up with them. Was that really you? There's no place to get film developed here.

Love,

Bobby B.

I wanted to ask him more about his grazing land in the mountains, but the next day he was asleep when I stopped by on my rounds. I left the latest issue of Mountaineering on his bed along with the paper.

Dear Margo,

I was at the front. It was bitter cold. The rest of them were dead. Our Wing B mailroom's down the hall. There was no end in sight. I saw nothing moving. The ammo had run out. Our mailman comes by in the morning. I was by myself. New snow covered up the bodies. I tried to stand up. We get mail six days a week. I couldn't hear a thing. My leg was numb. I was hungry. It was getting dark. You had the Victrola on. I wait for the mail. My canteen was frozen. On Sunday there's no mail. You said you'd always be with me, you said no matter what. I propped my back against a tree. Everything was still. My dog tags read blood type A plus, Presbyterian. Sometimes the mail is not on time. I pulled a picture out. Your mother went to bed and we were there all by themselves. It's delivered to the mailroom. I saw something move! Other faiths live at Spring Lake. I raised my M-1. They put the letters in our slots. A figure moved toward me! I count on the paper boy. Your hair touched my cheek. The figure stood before me! My slot is B-42. He looked like my father when my father was not sick. "Hi, Bobby," he said. "Pop?" I said. "You'll be okay," he said. Some of the other slots fill up. I lowered my M-1. "You'll make it, Bobby," he said. "She's watching. So is He." Sometimes there's something in my slot. "They're coming for you now." Last time it was for someone else. I looked up. Pop was gone! I heard the rumble of a convoy. The mail's late.

Yours,

B.

He must have been in the army, but he never talked about it. His letter to Margo says that he had an M-1, so it must have been back in World War II or Korea. I wrote to the Veterans Administration in Washington, D.C. to see what I could find out about him, but they never answered me. (They're like the phone company.)

I wanted to talk more with him about the mountain land, but the next day he wasn't in his room. I think that was a day they had taken him for more tests.

Dear Margo,

I read the paper every day. Cancer rates are up. The Lord is my shepherd. I shall not want. Nothing happened here last night. Native tribes are starving. I know psalms by heart. Divorces have reached record highs. Lightning killed a man. There was looting in the streets. Wing C is quarantined. He restoreth my soul. We had pancakes for breakfast. An avalanche buried a town. Someone's baby was abandoned. They found body parts. He leadeth me beside still waters. They abducted them. The death toll rises. They blame drugs. War has been declared. He leadeth me in the paths of righteousness. The streets are not safe. There's an epidemic. The National Guard is out. I will fear no evil, for Thou art with me. They have no antidote. Thou anointest my head with oil. Your mother made iced tea. Fire left a family homeless. The drought won't let up. I read the paper anyway. An earthquake buried them.

The paper boy reminds me of myself. Your cheek touched mine. Thou preparest a table before me. I hear cries down the hall. Thy rod and thy staff they comfort me. The flood took everything. Babies are born without fathers. It was dark out on the porch. Surely goodness and mercy shall follow me. A couple killed themselves. Crops were ruined. Banks foreclosed. They nailed Him to the cross. He maketh me to lie down in green pastures. You took me inside. I walk through the valley of the shadow of death. You're with me in the night. We have non-believers here. There is no peace in sight. Why does He let it happen? Has He sent the boy for us? I shall dwell in the house of the Lord forever. Amen.

Yours,

B.B.

The next day he was back in his room. "Have you got anything funny to read, boy?" he said. I found an old copy of Popeye Comics in my pile, and that was the first time I ever saw him smile.

He hadn't forgotten about a trip to the high grazing land. "Don't forget, boy, we're going out to the mountains," he said.

"Okay... Anytime," I said. (I never knew whether to call him mister or sir or by his first name, so I just didn't call him by any name at all.)

Dear Margo,

My Grandpa died. I don't feel good. The minister was there. I read our Health Newsletter. We were all dressed up. The paper boy will take me out there. Watch your weight, it says. I sat in back of you in class. Something hurts down here. I shook hands with grownups. Grandpa was laid out. I wrote a note to you in class. Take in good deep breaths. Grandpa's hands were folded. Miss Wright liked to call on you. It says to eat your vegetables. I'm weak but I can write. You wore glasses. I still liked you. Grandpa looked so white. Exercise three times a week. It hurts more when I move. Grandma hugged and kissed me. You were taller than the rest. I touched Grandpa's hand when no one watched. Milk makes strong bones. I knew Grandpa was in heaven. You have such dark eyes. I wake up thinking in the night and can't get back to sleep. It's hard to write when I don't feel good. The nurse is not here. I asked Grandpa to ask God to make you like me more. It says don't smoke. Eat fresh fruit. Keep fat intake low. I think my breakfast's coming up. Sleep eight hours a night. I just pushed the nurse-call button. Cut down on your salt. We were alone out on the porch. Rinse your fresh fruit off. I pushed again. It's getting worse. No one's coming yet. Please take it easy on the heart.

Yours forever,

B.

B – 42 Album
Handwriting on back of photo:
"10 years old – in her Sunday best."

He didn't look well at all the next day, but I could see that he wanted to tell me something.

"It's not too far, boy," he said.

I knew he was talking about the mountain land.

"Up in the Pioneer Range," he said. "We've got to get up there soon . . ."

Then he started coughing and wheezing and he couldn't stop. I called for the nurse, and sat him up straight in bed and slapped him on the back. By the time the nurse came he was better, and I had to go finish my rounds.

Dear Margo,

You didn't see me sitting back there. The houselights
were low. What would I do here without you and the paper
boy. It was the latest movie. You were with somebody else. I
hope that what I'm writing down is not too jumbled up. He got
drinks. Your hair was down. I feel better now. When I talk to
people here, the words don't sound like this. They put me on
oxygen. You turned to talk to him. The screen was starting to
light up. You had earrings on. He put his arm around you. I
could see it all. The movie was a Western. I get hot and then
I'm cold. A cowboy rode on into town. He touched your long
dark hair! The extra blankets keep me warm. You didn't seem
to mind. The cowboy rode up to her porch. She tinkered with
her blouse. The veterans' home would take me, but I like it at
Spring Lake. Is my writing readable? He tipped his hat. She
smiled. He reined his horse in and got off and walked up on the
porch. You wore lipstick. I kept watching. He reached out for

you! I can't remember some of the big words I used to know. She backed away. He took her arm. She tried to break loose. There was no one there to help. The cowboy held her tight. I leapt up! "Let go!" I yelled. "She's my girl! Keep away!" It all happened here last night. People turned and stared. The usher shined his flashlight. I slid down in my seat. This was before you knew that we would never end.

Love,

B.

The next day he looked better, but they had fitted him up with an oxygen inhaler under his nose and a portable tank by the bed.

"They say I need this, son," he said. "Soon as I can get this off, I'll be ready."

Dear Margo,

Last night was exam time. I hadn't been to class. They didn't say where the tests were. My glasses had been lost. The others were all ready. I didn't have the books. They put stronger light bulbs by my bed so I can read. I asked about the subjects. They kept rushing by. Last time I asked the doctor not to do my cataracts. There were no signs on the doors. I wondered where to go. An ophthalmologist comes once a month to Spring Lake Home. I saw you! "This way," you said. Tuition was not paid. I looked up ophthalmologist to make sure how it's spelled. The exams had started. My alarm clock didn't work. They told me that they'd only fix my eyes one at a time. You led me through a doorway. Everyone was at his desk. The doctor's light shined in my eyes. I found a place to sit. Your hair was in the ponytail. Someone said "You're late." He put a patch on one of my eyes. You sat next to me. A man gave me the questions. My pen was out of ink. The doctor pointed to the eye chart. I made letters up. You gave me a pencil. I wrote down my name. The doctor did the other eye. My pencil broke in half. I write large enough to read. You stayed by my side. I tried to read the questions, but the questions weren't in words. The boy gave me his magnifier. A bell rang up front. My sheet was blank. "Time's up," a man said. Everyone was done. The doctor ordered special glasses. A man stopped by me. You handed in my paper with the answers written out. They took me back to 42. My test score was A plus. I see at night without my glasses.

Yours forever,

B.

He took me by the arm when he saw me the next day. His oxygen inhaler was off and the tank was gone. "I've got a map to show you, son," he said.

He had it all drawn out on a sheet of paper. "The creek runs through it, right down through this meadow here," he said. "About an hour west."

"It's three sections, boy," he said. "Up by the high peaks. You better do the driving, son." (He was still calling me "son" or "boy," but I still didn't know what to call him.)

I tucked the map into my bag and decided to ask Grandma if I could borrow the old truck on Saturday night.

Dear Margo,

I was driving through the storm. The mountains weren't in sight. A painter came to paint my room. I was heading home. Pooch was curled up on the seat. The gas gauge was on full. They fixed the leak above the window. My tires still had tread. The painter spread his dropcloth. It got foggy out. We were alone on your front porch. Spring Lake hires its own men. The painter set his ladder up. I feel good today. The high meadow is surrounded by our snowcapped peaks. I watched him bring the paint in. Pooch woke up. She licked my face. I knew how to get there. It kept raining on and off. I asked if I could pick the color. The fog disappeared. I saw a church! We pulled over. It stood on a knoll. I jumped out. Pooch followed me. We trudged up through the sage. I saw a cross up on the steeple. All the paint was white. I looked in through a window. The painter mixed his paint. I couldn't see the mountains yet.

Pooch sniffed and she pawed. The door was open. I stepped in. The painter moved my bed. I fell asleep last night before I finished all my prayers. A wind came howling through the door. He did the ceiling first. The rain was stopping. I kneeled down. The sun was coming out! I saw them! Out beyond the plain. Our snowcapped mountain peaks! The painter moved my bed back. Our cottage is up there. White's okay for my room. It all happens when it's dark. Dear Margo, the boy's taking me. He's got the map.

Yours,

B.

Photo by Richard Blanchard
On the way to the high peaks

Care Giver

When I got home I checked his map against the state road map and made sure I knew how to get there. It looked like seventy miles or so out across the plains and over the pass to his spread under the high peaks.

The next afternoon I asked the nurse if it would be okay for me to take him out for a day trip. She said she was doubtful that she could get approval but that she would ask the doctor.

He was asleep when I got to his room, which just been repainted, and they had left his window open to help clear the paint fumes. It was cold in the room so I tiptoed over to the window to lower it, and I tested the latch to make sure it would be easy to open again.

Dear Margo,

Nothing happened last night! The doctor looked at me. My coffee tasted different. I am waiting for the boy. Do not fear, He sayeth. He shall deliver us. You took my hand. That's all for now.

Love forever,

B.

The next day the nurse shook her head when she saw me. "I asked the doc," she said. "I'm sorry. We can't take responsibility to let him go. He's not allowed to leave the Home in his condition. . . ."

I waited until my rounds were over and went back to his room when no one else was there, and then we made our plans for Saturday night.

Dear Margo,

You were in the garden. The boy and I made plans. Our cottage sat there by itself up near the snow-capped peaks. I breathed in the mountain air. Flowers were in bloom. Everything was as it should be. We were young and strong. Pooch played in the meadow. There was coffee on the stove. A trail led to the snowfields. It only rained at night. There were voices out there! I pushed the shutters back. The meadow ran down to the creek. What? I saw *a* <u>house</u>! Pooch was barking. I heard engines. This was ours alone. I pulled on a pair of boots. There were trucks outside! I heard chain saws starting up. There was <u>another</u> house! They were chopping down the trees that grow along the creek. I heard you calling to me! A dozer was out front! I saw more trucks! Where was my shotgun? I looked out again. A crane was hoisting up a billboard! I got to the door. Men were pouring concrete pavement up to our front steps! I lurched forward. My legs buckled. Concrete filled my boots. I didn't know where you were. The men would not stop. Dear Margo, last night was a nightmare. They tore down the cross. The boy and I are going back to make sure.

Yours,

B.B.

On Saturday night I parked the truck out behind Wing B near his window and turned the engine off and waited until lights out. It was a clear night with a full moon, just what we had hoped for. I had left his window unlatched and a crack open when I was in his room that afternoon, so I could pull up the window from the outside and crawl back in without any trouble. (In case anyone had seen me outside the window or in his room, I was going to say that I had come back to get my school bag).

He was wide awake and he was all dressed under the covers. I got him up and sat him down on his chair. Then I took the extra blankets from the closet and I stuffed them under the covers to make it look like he was still in bed. Between the two of us, we got him out through the open window and into the bushes. (I thanked The Lord that his room was on the ground floor.) Then we hobbled along with his arm over my shoulder until we made it to the truck.

It was more than an hour's drive across the sage plains on past the abandoned church and then up over the pass and up the long dirt road through the cattle guards and on up toward the high meadow above the little valley. We bounced along under the full moon and he sat in the cab without saying anything except to tell me where to turn. He had his special glasses on and I saw that he kept looking out at the country which he hadn't seen first-hand for a long time.

We shifted into low up the two-track road into the high meadow. When we got up to a level spot behind a little knoll he said "Right here, son," so that's where we stopped. We rolled down the truck windows and I shut the engine off.

With the full moon, it was light enough to see everything. There was a spring just above us, and a little creek ran on down through the meadow past the truck. I could see snowfields on the high peaks up above. "Set me down here, son," he said, and so I lifted him down out of the truck and sat him down on the cool meadow grass. I propped his back against my rucksack and wrapped a coat around him and we stayed up there together, sitting side by side. "Here's where the cottage goes, son," he said, and then he was quiet. I stared up at the high peaks and the moon and the stars and tried not to think about the weekend homework I hadn't done.

We made it back before daybreak, back in through the B-42 window at the Spring Lake Home. I took off his shoes, folded the extra blankets back into the closet, got him into bed with his clothes still on, and pulled the covers up over him. All he said was "Thanks, son" and fell sound asleep before I crawled back out through the window.

Then I had to make it home without Grandma seeing me come in. But she was waiting for me at the kitchen door.

Dear Margo,

Almost all the work was done. I heard someone knock. You were outside in the garden. Pooch barked at the door. I said "I can't believe it! Pop?" "Hello, Bob," Pop said. "Pop, you found us!" I said. He came through the cottage door. Pop wasn't old and crippled. We sat down in the big room. Snowcapped peaks were all around us. It was springtime out. An antelope stood watching. The meadow was in bloom. "We've got everything," I said. "There's nothing else to need." Pooch jumped up. She licked Pop's hand. "We built it, Pop," I said. The creek was running clear and deep. The sun shone through the trees. Pop nodded. "Every night is cool. We're never sick," I said. We had enough wood stacked out back to last us all year long. I called you. "Pop," I said. "Can you stay here with us?" I stoked up the fireplace. Cattle grazed down by the creek. "The trail goes to the snowfields," I said. "We climb way up there." Pop did not look any older than I was last night. I saw you coming from the garden. Pooch ran out to you. "The snowfields never melt," I said. We didn't need a clock. My left arm won't move today. The doctor's coming in. I am thankful for the boy.

Yours forever,

B.

I had to tell Grandma about him and about where we had gone on Saturday night. I showed her his map to prove it. After thinking about what happened, Grandma said I had done the right thing for the old man, but she took my allowance away and made me stay home because I had gone out all night without permission. It was Sunday so I wasn't missing school, but I didn't get to make my rounds at Spring Lake Home that day.

Dear Margo,

They put me on a stretcher. Thank Lord I can write this out. Your mother made iced tea for us. New doctors looked at me. They wheeled me in. I held my cross. You put music on. I got moved onto the table. The porch light was out. I saw gauges, levers, tubes. The room was spic and span. They hooked something up to me. Your mother was upstairs. "Start counting down from ten," they said. The light was in my eyes. You were in your summer blouse. "Ten, nine, eight," I said. Men in gowns were all around me. "Seven, five," I said. You put my hand behind your back. They said it wouldn't hurt. "Three," I said. "Like this," you said. Your breath was sweet mint tea. Stars were out. I stopped counting. The next song was on. "Patient under," someone said. I had my eyes shut tight. You put your arm around me. They were all gloved up. I made believe I was unconscious. "Insert scope," I heard. They said it was exploratory. Your cheek touched my cheek. School was over for the summer. Your lips touched my face. I was watching everything from just above their heads. It didn't hurt. You whispered to me. I kept watching them. You took my hand. They kept going. I saw everything. "I'll be with you," you said. Now I'm back in my room. The left arm still won't work. The boy was here.

Love,

Bobby B.

When I got back to Spring Lake Home on Monday, the nurse told me that they thought he had had a stroke but that now he was back in his room, so I went directly to B-42. He was laying there in bed, staring up at the ceiling.

"Are you okay?" I said.

"Can't move the left . . . boy," he said. His words sounded slurred, but I could still understand most of what he said. "They keep asking why . . . all dressed under the covers. . . ." I think he tried to say.

He had a pad and pencil next to him on the bed, and he pointed to the blank paper with his good hand. "Put . . . name and address here, son. . . ." I heard him say. So I printed my name and address on the pad and set it back on the bed.

Dear Margo,

Last night was my birthday. I remember everything. My left side isn't working now but I write with my right. I know you were here last night. Pop died in sixty-six. The paper boy is a good boy. VE Day is May 8th. Pop was on December 1. You are September 9. How could it be Alzheimer's? I know the doctors' names. You brought me a birthday cake. Gramp died in thirty-eight. You were wearing the blue dress and you put lipstick on. Gramp had a stroke and wouldn't eat. Pop said they let him go. I know that I repeat myself, but that is what I do. "Happy Birthday, Bobby," you said. I am eighty-one. They say that long-term memory is the very last to go. "Make a wish!" you said. Mom died when we were born. I made the only wish I make. Our father brought us up. I took a breath. There was one candle. I blew. It went out. You were only twenty-one. Our place is still safe. "I'm yours, Bobby," you said. My only wish came true! He lets you visit after hours.

Yours forever,

B.

The next day his words were slurred even more and he said his whole left side was numb. I think he said he had just had another birthday and that she had come to see him. (I didn't know who he meant back then.)

He didn't try to say anything else for a little while, and then he pulled me close with his good arm. "Listen son," he said clearly. "... Will you make ... a promise?"

"Yes ... sure," I said.

"When ... time comes, son, make sure ... let me go."

I knew what he meant, and I didn't know what to say.

When I left I asked the nurse whether anyone had signed the visitors register to come to see him. She looked, and shook her head no. (I do remember seeing the leftovers from a cake and a candle in his room.)

Dear Margo,

I went up to heaven! God was there! I was a boy. Miss Wright marked me absent. I had to pinch myself. Snow-capped peaks were all around us. He wore clothes like ours. I swear on The Bible. I could talk to Him. We strolled through the meadow. I don't always say my prayers. He read my mind! "It's alright," He said. I was not afraid. We didn't use words when we talked. It was sunny out. We sat down beside the creek. My homework wasn't done. "You've got time," He said. I've missed Sunday School. He didn't have a beard and robes the way I thought He would. Birds were singing in the trees. My shoes were untied. I peeked over at the answers to our grammar test. "I know," He said. My shirt was untucked. I've said dirty words. God didn't look old but He must be. Flowers were in bloom. Antelope drank from the creek. God knows who I am. It wasn't cold and wasn't hot. He said He's in my heart. I worked up my courage. A cross was by the path. "My Lord," I said. "Am I allowed to bring somebody else?" He knew who I was thinking of. The sky was heaven blue. He said we both belong. They'll say I made this up.

Love,

B.

He looked a little better the next day. "Don't forget, son...", I heard him say.

As I was finishing my rounds that afternoon, I saw the Spring Lake Home administrator and his secretary coming out of B-42 with some folders in their hands.

Dear Margo,

I ...

(There was nothing else written on this sheet in his notebook.)

When I came in the next day he was laying there in bed curled up like a baby. I think he tried to say hello but he couldn't make a sound. His face was rigid when he tried to talk, and his mouth was twisted off to one side. All he could do was lift his right arm and take my hand. I called the nurse, and when she saw him she called the doctor. I waited until the doctor came, and then they asked me to leave.

Dear Margo,

What is this new room we're in? I try to talk but can't. The Gospel's going through my head. Can you read what I write? They've got me plugged into machines. I'll try to make you smile. Miss Wright wrote euthanasia: I said teenagers, Hong Kong. He hath promised life eternal. My right hand still works. There are tubes and needles going into both my arms. Your mother made iced tea for us. Whosoever doth believe. God giveth us forever after. I can't feel one side. We were alone out on the porch. Please wear your white blouse. I asked Him and He answered yes, the boy's our what-will-be. Doctors come and doctors go. I see your brown eyes. Thou shalt never perish. The boy knows what to do. Hold my hand. We were alone. You do my everything. Please don't forget about the boy.

Yours forever,

B.

He wasn't in his room, and they wouldn't let me see him. All I could find out was that they had moved him to the Special Care Unit and that his condition was critical. (The nurse did tell me that he wouldn't let go of his pencil and his notebook when they loaded him on the stretcher.)

Now I read again what he wrote to her. "I asked Him and He answered yes, the boy's our what-will-be."

Dear Margo,

I was right there with him. Pop was breathing fast. The doctor said that there was nothing more that they could do. The tubes are still hooked up to me. It doesn't even hurt. I'm bound and determined to get all this written down. Needles are taped to my arms. I'm writing anyway. My chair was pulled up to Pop's bed. We were all alone. They come to examine me. Pop's tubes got tangled up. You said you'd never leave me. I had his hand in mine. Pop would put me on his shoulders. I count my heart beats. They say the average life span's up to almost eighty now. I couldn't think of what to say. Someone checks my pulse. He read to me before lights-out. Your cheek touched my face. Pop was a good soldier. A new doctor read my chart. Pop's hand was cold. They tried to feed me. My mouth is so dry. Pop took me to the mountains. He said "Keep on going, son!" Should I have told Pop he'd get well? They try to make me drink. It is hard to write like this. Pop fought at the front. He kicked in the steps so I could make it to the top. They flex my legs. Pop won medals. Soldiers don't complain. They hooked new bottles to my tubes. His eyes were open wide. Pop said "Stand up good and straight, son." His hand squeezed me tight. Pop gave me his medals. I was just a PFC. I fixed Pop's pillow for him. He said "You can do it, son." Should I have told him that I love him? We don't talk like that. I was sitting at attention. I pulled Pop's tubes out. He hath promised life eternal. Pop's hand went slack.

Yours,

B.

They still wouldn't let me in to see him. They told me he was still in critical condition. (He was trying so hard to keep writing no matter what!)

Dear Margo,

I can't remember. Please stay with me. My left side won't move. They must have given me more drugs.

Yours forever,

B.

I asked again. They said I'm not allowed to see him because I'm not kin. I remembered that the office had told me that Margo Jones was listed as next of kin, but that no address was written in after her name.

Dear Margo,

"Bobby?" you said. "Yes?" I said. "I'm not afraid," you said. Can you read my writing? A different nurse is on. All was quiet in the house. My right arm still works. Can you hear what I am thinking? Your lips touched my cheek. "Bobby?" you said to me. Another doctor came. "Do you think Mom's asleep?" you said. School was over now. The doctor's calling for more tests. My words do not come out. I took a sip of sweet mint tea. Your eyes were Margo brown. They put new tubes into me. You had me by the hand. A breeze was coming through your window. The nurse propped me up. "Bobby? " you said. "Let me." I can't feel my other side. You did the unbuttoning. I heard the doctors talk. They wrote out instructions. I try to lie still. Your skin was just a little lighter where the swim suit was. "Margo...". It was summertime. I don't know the words. Everything that ever happens is still here and now. They probed in with instruments. I concentrate on you. Lord, please let joy come to all. Don't ever go away. "Do you feel this?" they said. I shook my head for no. You are God's most lovely creature brought down here to earth. They tried again. I shook my head. The two of us are one. "I'll never leave you, Bobby, ever," you said. "You will see!" That is what you said to me. They made marks on my chart. "Can you feel this? Or this?" they said. I'm waiting.

Love,

B.B.

I tried to get in to the Special Care Unit through the delivery door, but it was locked. I knew that if I pushed the buzzer and someone came to the door, they wouldn't let me in. I had to think of something else.

Dear Margo,

It was our celebration. You sat close. I had Pop's car. The Lord is my shepherd, I shall not want. You said yes to me. You ran your fingers through my hair. We were on our way. Surely goodness and mercy shall follow us. It was snowing hard. You held the ring for me to see. I wasn't slowing down. "We'll have a garden," you said. I had the defroster on. "Up in the high meadow." Something came around the curve. I turned up the wipers. The lights were in my eyes! We hadn't set the date yet. I slammed down on the brakes. It was coming at us! I swerved! We were off the road. I don't know how long we'd been there. Our lights were still on. I couldn't tell which way was up. I smelled gasoline. There you were! "Margo!" I can taste blood now. Your eyes were open. "Margo!" There was not a sound. You weren't moving! I edged closer. Snowflakes drifted in. Lord help us! "Margo, say something!" You slumped down. It went dark. Dear Margo, I've stopped eating. The good hand still works. I see signs of the cross no matter where I look.

Yours,

B.

B – 42 Album
No identification

Care Giver

I found out which room he was in by calling the Special Care Unit nursing station and telling them there was a flower delivery. It worked.

Dear Margo,

We made it up there! I could walk. I talked! No aches! No pains! Our creek was running clear and full. My writing hand's okay. You were picking flowers. My hair was brown again. Our cottage sat by the high meadow. "Thank you, Lord," I said. There weren't any other houses! It was sunny out. Dewdrops sparkled. Birds were singing. You were almost due. The breeze was light. I tossed a stick. Pooch went after it. Snowcapped peaks rose up on high. Pop was chopping wood. We met on the meadow path. You put your hand in mine. "He's kicking, Bobby! Feel this!" you said. It was spring up there. A cross stood in among the blossoms. Your hand slipped away. Storm clouds rolled in out of nowhere and you disappeared! What happened? I was back in bed. I'm old. I'm pale. I'm weak. A doctor stood there over me. They put needles in. It was dark out. "Lord," I said. "Please let us go back." There were other people crowding in around my bed. I tried to speak. Thy kingdom come. They took my covers off. I heard you! "Bobby," you were saying. "It will be okay." I keep trying to write this. They asked me to stop. The boy is coming to help us. I'm ready now.

Love,

B.

I got in there late at night. The window wasn't locked. He was there all by himself, hooked up to a machine. I closed the door. He was awake. I turned the bed light on. He tried to move his arm but couldn't. Then I held his hand. He could not speak. I said a prayer. The time had come for us. READY he said with his eyes. It was as it should be. I disconnected tubes and wires. "Thanks, boy," he almost said. I made it back to my room without Grandma waking up.

According to the records at the Spring Lake Home, Robert A. Brown passed away sometime after midnight on December twenty-first, as reported by the Special Care Unit night nurse.

The chaplain said the twenty-third psalm under a little tent in the cemetery behind the Presbyterian Church. Only four of us were there; the night nurse, the rehab instructor, the Spring Lake administrator, and I. Then I saw someone else - a tall young woman with dark hair standing beside me. She said "Hello, John." She reached out and touched my arm and then she kissed my cheek. The chaplain said "Let us pray," and I bowed my head. When I looked up again, she was gone.

Photograph by Richard Blanchard
On the road to the high peaks

Care Giver

It was delivered to Grandma's house by Certified Mail, Return Receipt Requested.

It was the Last Will and Testament signed by Robert A. Brown, witnessed by the administrator of the Spring Lake Home and notarized by the administration secretary. It said "I hereby bequeath unto John Fulton, a minor . . . all my worldly goods and possessions . . . including all those grazing lands described in Deed Book 12 pages 8-11 . . . and my. . ."

Dear Margo,

I know you were standing by me. They've closed Spring Lake Home. At last I've got this put together and all written down. The high meadow is in bloom. Grandma's up in years. I don't have any place to send this. Please come back.

Yours,

John

Care Giver

*Notation on back of photo: Spring Lake
Home after closing.*

*This photograph and those appearing
on pages 137, 139, 141, 143, 145, 147,
and 149 were found among John
Fulton's possessions.*

Dear Margo,

I've got the cottage staked out. Grandma needs more tending to. I'm taking snapshots for you. The herd's grazing down below. He hath promised life eternal. The snow's deep in the high peaks. Please surprise me. I'll be here.

Yours forever,

John

Dear Margo,

The doctor says she's losing ground. We dug the basement out. Does He let you decide how young or old you'd like to be? Please stay just the way you are. Good men are helping us. We'll see the high peaks from our bedroom.

Yours forever,

John

Dear Margo,

I'm sorry for poor Grandma. Our fireplace walls are up. I climb the trail to the high peaks to be up close to Him. You put my hand behind your back. We sipped sweet mint tea. A cross appeared up on the chimney in the night.

Yours,

John

Dear Margo,

Grandma can't walk any more. I cook. I wash. I clean. We're starting on the cottage walls. You stood close to me. Grandma's life's no life to live now. He shall raise thee up. We'll be all closed in for winter. Please come soon.

Yours,

John

Dear Margo,

Grandma says He says it's time. I wait until it's dark. The walls are up, the roof is on, we beat the winter storms. Please pray for her peace of mind. The firewood's split and stacked. I see you with him in one snapshot. Pooch is with you, too. The snow is deep. It's warm inside. We get the morning sun. I bought a nightgown for you.

Yours forever,

John

Dear Margo,

It's done now. We had services. God bless Grandma's soul. The walls are chinked. Our fence line needs work. We were by ourselves. He hath promised life forever. Your mother was upstairs. I put the Christmas tree up for us.

Yours forever,

John

Dear Margo,

He said I am our what-will-be. It's all ready now. I switch off the porch light and put the Victrola on. Everything is here for us. The creek is running full. Last night I dreamt that I was climbing up to where you are. Are you really coming? Should I go to you? I can see the snowfields in the moonlight from down here. Are you there? You took my hand. Should I start climbing now? I'll wait a little longer. Your lips touched my cheek.

Love,

John

Publisher's Note

The notes, photographs, and letters in this volume were assembled and edited by Richard Blanchard. They were found at the Fulton cottage by the Custer County authorities, who were alerted to investigate after John Fulton's mail remained uncollected for seven weeks. According to the sheriff's report, his truck was found parked outside the cottage. Nothing in the cottage appeared to be disturbed. John Fulton (single, 23) is now listed as a missing person.

photograph by Richard Blanchard
The cottage door

Richard Blanchard is the author of *The High Traverse*, and his short stories have appeared in *The Quarterly*. He was born in New Jersey and now divides his time between Idaho and the Northeast. This is his second novel.